W9-BJU-965

DATE DUE

DATE DUE
DATE DUE
DATE DUE
DATE DUE
DATE DUE
DATE DUE
DATE DUE

All in a Day

by Mitsumasa Anno

and

Raymond Briggs

Ron Brooks

Eric Carle

Gian Calvi

Zhu Chengliang

Leo and Diane Dillon

Akiko Hayashi

Nicolai Ye. Popov

Philomel Books • New York

The publishers gratefully acknowledge
the assistance of Kazuko Shiraishi and Susan Tsumura in
the translation of the text for this book.

First U.S.A. edition 1986. Published by Philomel Books, a member of
The Putnam Publishing Group, 51 Madison Avenue, New York, N.Y. 10010.

Library of Congress Cataloging-in-Publication Data Anno, Mitsumasa, Date. All in a day. Translation of: Marui chikyū no maru ichinichi. Summary: Brief text and illustrations by ten internationally well-known artists reveal a day in the lives of children in eight different countries showing the similarities and differences and emphasizing the commonality of humankind. [1. Brotherliness—Fiction] I. Briggs, Raymond et al. II. Title. PZ7.A5875A1 1986 [E] 86-5011
ISBN 0-399-21311-2

A Few Words to the Readers of This Book

Next door to the country you live in, there is another country where children also live. And beyond that next-door country, there is still another country with children in it as well. In all of these countries throughout the world there are many, many children, all of whom, like you, want to grow up as soon as possible. Or so we suppose.

While you are out playing, some children are fast asleep in a far-off land. While you are building a snowman, some other children somewhere else are swimming in the sea. At any one moment, children all over the world are having these and many other experiences, as you can see in the pictures in this book.

Since the places we live in are different, the colors of our skin, the shapes of our houses, the clothes we wear, and the words we speak may well be different, too. But the expressions on our faces and the sounds of our voices when we laugh or cry are very much the same, no matter where we live. On the night that the moon looks round to you, it is the same full moon all over the world. And it is a fact that the sun is the same one-and-only sun to everyone in the world.

Actually, in all the great universe, there is only one planet, the earth, where people can live, and we all live on it together. It is hard to say why this should be so. But we have made this book with the hope that by the time you grow up and learn more about such things, this earth will have become a better place for you to live on, a place where everyone is always happy and friendly.

From all the People Who Made This Book

U.S.A. (Chicago) *December 31, 6 p.m. (18:00)*

SOS! SOS! I have been shipwrecked on this island.
On the map it is called "Uninhabited Island."
Sailor Oliver Smith is my name, but they call me SOS.
Zé of Brazil, stop making kites. Come and save me!
What? You are about to go to sleep? But it's just
12 noon here. Well, good night, then. *Boa noite!*

Brazil (Rio de Janeiro) *December 31, 10 p.m. (22:00)*

England (Greenwich) *January 1, 0 a.m. (0:00)*

Kae-Kae of China, Happy New Year! *Xinnian hao!*
You and your friends have so many pretty clothes!
All I have is one shirt and what I have on.
Please put down your firecrackers and save me!
I'm catching a fish for my dinner, while Alyosha
of the Soviet Union dreams of a great feast.

Kenya (Nakuru) *January 1, 3 a.m. (3:00)*

U.S.S.R. (Moscow) *January 1, 3 a.m. (3:00)*

Japan (Tokyo) *January 1, 9 a.m. (9:00)*

Uninhabited Island *January 1, 12 noon (12:00)*

SOS's Uninhabited Island is in the South Pacific, somewhere near the International Date Line.

China (Beijing) *January 1, 8 a.m. (8:00)*

Australia (Sydney) *January 1, 11 a.m. (11:00)*

U.S.A. (Chicago) *December 31, 9 p.m. (21:00)*

England (Greenwich) *January 1, 3 a.m. (3:00)*

It's New Year's Eve in the U.S.A. but it's three o'clock in the afternoon here in the middle of the Pacific Ocean. Tom's mother is saying, "Good night, sleep tight." Then, when all the children fall asleep, the adults will have a big party. I know all about that!

Alyosha of the Soviet Union is still dreaming. Wake up! It's morning now. *Dobroe utro!* Something good is waiting for you today, Alyosha. I know all about that, too. But what about me? Hey, this is SOS, calling "SOS!"

Brazil (Rio de Janeiro) *January 1, 1 a.m. (1:00)*

Kenya (Nakuru) *January 1, 6 a.m. (6:00)*

U.S.S.R. (Moscow) *January 1, 6 a.m. (6:00)*

Japan (Tokyo) *January 1, 12 noon (12:00)*

Uninhabited Island *January 1, 3 p.m. (15:00)*

China (Beijing) *January 1, 11 a.m. (11:00)*

Australia (Sydney) *January 1, 2 p.m. (14:00)*

U.S.A. (Chicago) *January 1, 0 a.m. (0:00)*

England (Greenwich) *January 1, 6 a.m. (6:00)*

James of England, this is SOS calling.
Good morning, and a Happy New Year to you!
Is that "Reveille" you are playing on your trumpet?
Your mother doesn't seem to appreciate music,
but I like it a lot.

Jomo of Kenya,
good morning. *Umelalaje.*
And a Happy New Year to you!
Are you going to the market with your father?
He will buy a big melon for you, I am sure.

Brazil (Rio de Janeiro) *January 1, 4 a.m. (4:00)*

Kenya (Nakuru) *January 1, 9 a.m. (9:00)*

U.S.S.R. (Moscow) *January 1, 9 a.m. (9:00)*

Japan (Tokyo) *January 1, 3 p.m. (15:00)*

Uninhabited Island *January 1, 6 p.m. (18:00)*

China (Beijing) *January 1, 2 p.m. (14:00)*

Australia (Sydney) *January 1, 5 p.m. (17:00)*

U.S.A. (Chicago) *January 1, 3 a.m. (3:00)*

England (Greenwich) *January 1, 9 a.m. (9:00)*

Good day, Zé. *Bom dia.*
And a Happy New Year too! *Feliz Ano Novo!*
Last night you were dreaming about flying your kite. Now you can really do it.
Oh, I should have flown a kite painted "SOS!"

Ben of Australia, Happy New Year!
You are camping out tonight?
I've been camping out all the time, since no one comes to rescue me. I've made a TV set. I'll watch the crab dance for a while, then I'll go to sleep.

Brazil (Rio de Janeiro) *January 1, 7 a.m. (7:00)*

Kenya (Nakuru) *January 1, 12 noon (12:00)*

U.S.S.R. (Moscow) *January 1, 12 noon (12:00)*

Japan (Tokyo) *January 1, 6 p.m. (18:00)*

Uninhabited Island *January 1, 9 p.m. (21:00)*

China (Beijing) *January 1, 5 p.m. (17:00)*

Australia (Sydney) *January 1, 8 p.m. (20:00)*

U.S.A. (Chicago) *January 1, 6 a.m. (6:00)*

England (Greenwich) *January 1, 12 noon (12:00)*

Tom, this is the dog, Matey, calling.
Your kitty says it's time for you to wake up.
It's six in the morning in the U.S.A. where you live. Good morning! And Happy New Year!
It's midnight here on the island.
SOS has gone to sleep, so I'm calling instead.

Aki of Japan, this is me, Matey.
You look worried. You've lost your precious shuttlecock birdie, and your kitten Ranmaru hasn't come back yet. But it's eleven o'clock—time to go to sleep. You'll find them tomorrow.
Good night. *Oyasuminasai.*

Brazil (Rio de Janeiro) *January 1, 10 a.m. (10:00)*

Kenya (Nakuru) *January 1, 3 p.m. (15:00)*

U.S.S.R. (Moscow) *January 1, 3 p.m. (15:00)*

Japan (Tokyo) *January 1, 9 p.m. (21:00)*

Uninhabited Island *January 2, 0 a.m. (0:00)*

China (Beijing) *January 1, 8 p.m. (20:00)*

Australia (Sydney) *January 1, 11 p.m. (23:00)*

U.S.A. (Chicago) *January 1, 9 a.m. (9:00)*

England (Greenwich) *January 1, 3 p.m. (15:00)*

SOS . . . This is SOS. Kae-Kae, good night, *hao hao shie-ba.*
It's past your bedtime. You've stayed up late,
watching the New Year's fireworks.
Zé and his friends are flying kites.
Kae-Kae, I bet you're good at kite-flying, too.

Why in the world is Alyosha riding a bicycle
in the snow? Oops! See what happened!
He should have a sled, like Tom.
This is SOS. Dove, I've written an SOS letter.
I am counting on you to bring help for me.

Brazil (Rio de Janeiro) *January 1, 1 p.m. (13:00)*

Kenya (Nakuru) *January 1, 6 p.m. (18:00)*

U.S.S.R. (Moscow) *January 1, 6 p.m. (18:00)*

Japan (Tokyo) *January 2, 0 a.m. (0:00)*

Uninhabited Island *January 2, 3 a.m. (3:00)*

China (Beijing) *January 1, 11 p.m. (23:00)*

Australia (Sydney) *January 2, 2 a.m. (2:00)*

U.S.A. (Chicago) *January 1, 12 noon (12:00)*

Alyosha, you were so happy about your new bicycle that you rode it all over, even in the snow. And now, while you are sleeping, your bicycle is still close to you, beside your bed. Sweet dreams, Alyosha. Good night. *Dobroj nochi.*

Brazil (Rio de Janeiro) *January 1, 4 p.m. (16:00)*

England (Greenwich) *January 1, 6 p.m. (18:00)*

Jomo, good night to you, too. *Lala salama.*
It would be wonderful if you could ride that pink flamingo to visit me on my island.
Oh, look! I think my dove has reached Australia!
Is Ben coming to save me? Or is he just dreaming?

Kenya (Nakuru) *January 1, 9 p.m. (21:00)*

U.S.S.R. (Moscow) *January 1, 9 p.m. (21:00)*

Japan (Tokyo) *January 2, 3 a.m. (3:00)*

Uninhabited Island *January 2, 6 a.m. (6:00)*

China (Beijing) *January 2, 2 a.m. (2:00)*

Australia (Sydney) *January 2, 5 a.m. (5:00)*

U.S.A. (Chicago) *January 1, 3 p.m. (15:00)*

England (Greenwich) *January 1, 9 p.m. (21:00)*

Good night, James. It's your bedtime in England.
Tom is reading an exciting book in the U.S.A.
Aki is still sound asleep in Japan.
And both Alyosha and Kae-Kae are flying through the sky in their dreams.

Jomo is dreaming, too, but he dreams of lions.
Ben and his sister have breakfast on the beach,
while Zé and his brother walk home for supper.
What time is it in your town now? You can imagine what children of other lands are doing now, can't you?

Brazil (Rio de Janeiro) *January 1, 7 p.m. (19:00)*

Kenya (Nakuru) *January 1, 0 a.m. (0:00)*

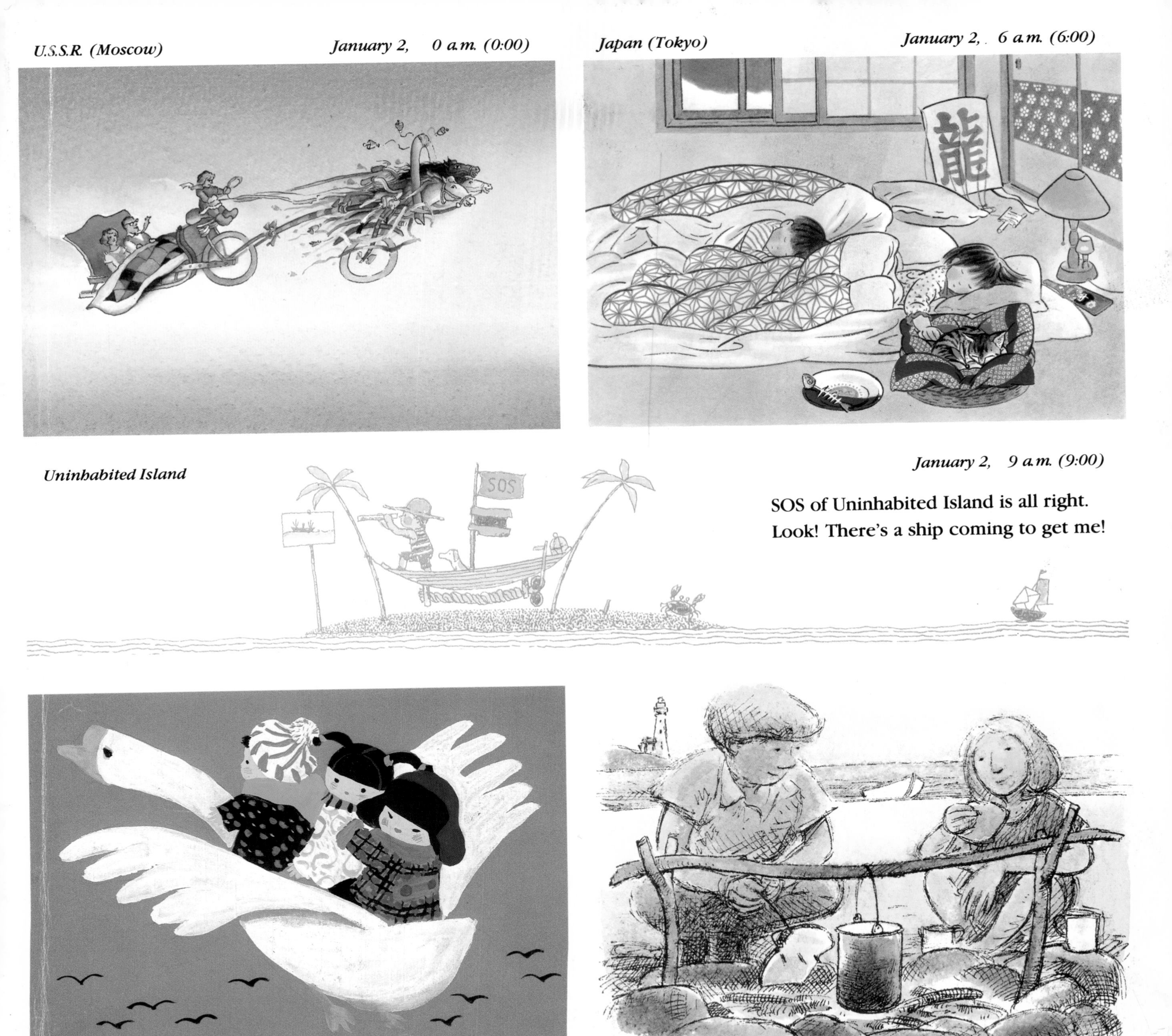

U.S.S.R. (Moscow) *January 2, 0 a.m. (0:00)*

Japan (Tokyo) *January 2, 6 a.m. (6:00)*

Uninhabited Island *January 2, 9 a.m. (9:00)*

SOS of Uninhabited Island is all right.
Look! There's a ship coming to get me!

China (Beijing) *January 2, 5 a.m. (5:00)*

Australia (Sydney) *January 2, 8 a.m. (8:00)*

A Note to Parents and Other Older Readers

Peace is the theme of this book, and the principal message that the authors hope young readers will find in it is that, despite many apparent differences, we are more like than unlike our neighbors all around the world, and we share their hopes for a peaceful and happy future for all who live on this, our mutual and only earth.

But as we observe children in many lands at the same moment, we see that their activities are related to the very different conditions of time and climate that exist in various parts of the earth. Readers may wonder why it is daytime in Chicago when it is nighttime in Beijing. And why is it winter in Tokyo when it is summer in Sydney? And why do people have different features and different skin colors in various parts of the globe?

It would take a much longer book than this one to answer all these questions completely. But it may be useful to explain some of the scientific principles that are touched on here.

Daylight and darkness are, of course, the results of sunlight falling on the earth, which is spinning on its own axis. As it rotates, the part that is facing the sun has daylight; the other part is covered by the shadow of night. As the earth turns, different parts of it move into and out of the sunlight. We say that the sun rises and sets, but in reality the sun is not moving—it is the turning of the earth that creates this illusion. It takes the earth 24 hours or 1 day to rotate once completely.

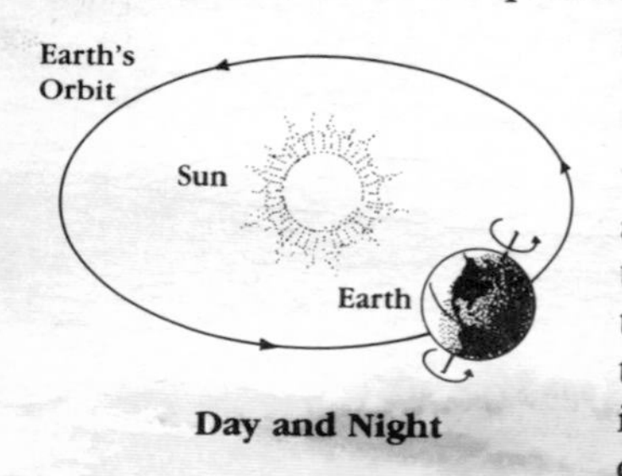

Day and Night

We call this 24-hour period a day, but why is a day divided into 24 hours? What is time, anyhow? The answer to the second question is a difficult and philosophical one, but the first is easily answered: People just decided that it was necessary to agree on some system of marking the passage of the seasons and measuring the days. They used many different systems before they really agreed on the one we use now. To put it simply, they thought of the earth as divided into 24 longitudinal sections, like the slices of an orange, each 15° wide. These sections were called time zones. As the sun at its highest point passed over each of these sections in turn, it was considered to be noon, or 12 o'clock, in that time zone. All the other hours of the day followed in sequence. The period of time it takes for the sun to move 15° from one section to the next was called an hour. Time moves westward by one hour every 15° of longitude, following the sun. So, for instance, it may be noon in New York, but it will not be noon in California for three more hours.

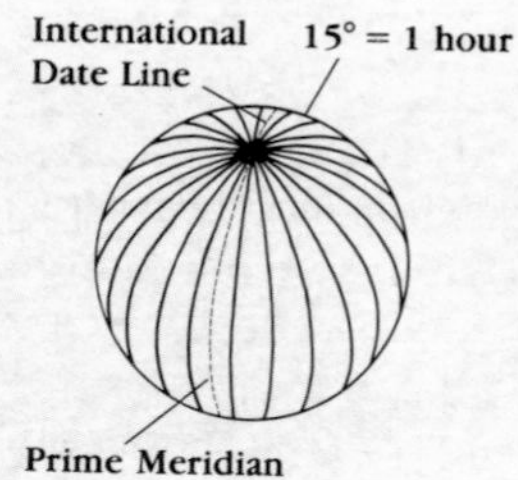

However, this system was still not completely convenient, especially since each country thought that its own capital city should be the official starting point for the measurement of time. Finally it was agreed that Greenwich Observatory in England would be considered the official beginning point. Now all other times could be described as being, say, Greenwich time plus five hours, or Greenwich time minus seven hours, and so on, and everyone would know exactly what time was meant by that. But it was still not convenient to have the time zones be so rigidly delineated. So the nations of the world have set up the time zones that are shown in this map. (Notice that

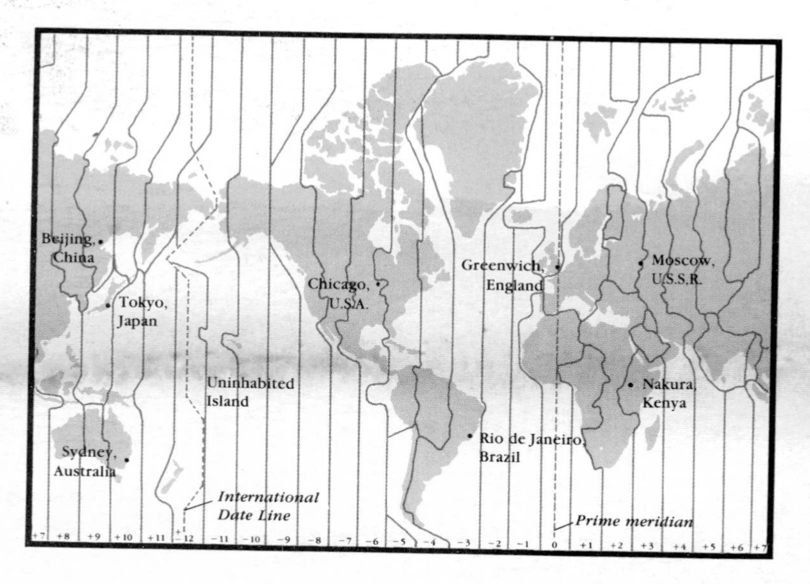

World Time Zones

where + 12 hours and − 12 hours meet an adjustment must be made. Their meeting point is called the International Date Line, and travelers who cross it gain or lose an entire day.)

In making the pictures for this book, it was decided to feature children in each of eight different time zones, some in the Northern Hemisphere and some in the Southern Hemisphere. Each double-page spread shows what time and season it is at one single moment in each of these eight places. Then we have shown, on successive double spreads, what children would be doing in each of these places three hours later, then six, nine, twelve, fifteen, eighteen and twenty-one hours later. Greenwich Mean Time was used as the base, so the first picture shows the time there as 0:00 on January 1, the beginning of a day at the beginning of a year. At that moment, you can see that English children are sound asleep in the winter night, but it is 11 o'clock in a sunny summer's morning in Sydney, Australia, and children there are getting ready to go on a beach picnic. (In this book, standard time is used in the countries in the Northern Hemisphere, but it is summer in January in Brazil and Australia, and so the time shown in these countries is standard time plus one hour, like our "daylight saving time.")

Although the day is divided into 24 hours, your clock probably shows only the first 12, and repeats them after noon. But some people now use a 24-hour system in telling time. So, rather than saying that it is 10:00 in the morning or 10:00 in the evening, they would use 10:00 to mean only the morning hour, and use 22:00 to signify the corresponding evening hour. Many travelers have watches or clocks that use this system, and some of these have an extra, movable rim that can be turned to show the time in other parts of the world. Airlines, too, use the 24-hour schedule. Yet most of us still use 12-hour clocks. So you can see that even today we have not really agreed completely on how to tell time!

In fact, it would be perfectly possible to invent some other system entirely for measuring time. We could, for example, decide to have it be the same time simultaneously all over the earth. In many ways this might be more convenient than the present system. Perhaps you can think of some other ways to measure time.

By now it is clear why it is night on one side of the earth and day on the opposite side, but why is it winter in one place and summer somewhere else? It is sunlight that makes the seasons, too. The diagram below shows that while the earth turns completely around on its axis in one day, it also revolves around the sun, taking a year to make the journey. As the earth makes its year-long revolution around the sun, different parts of its surface remain longer in the full light of the sun, or are moved away from the sun's light for longer periods, making parts of the earth warmer and cooler accordingly. We call these periods of warmth and cold, and the periods in between, the seasons.

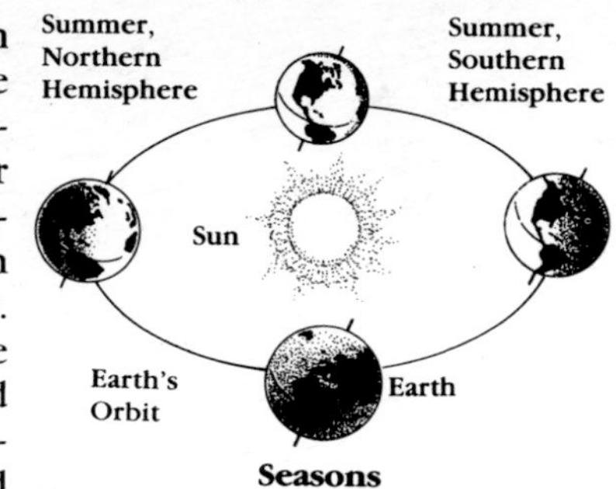

Seasons

Around the middle of the earth is an (imaginary) line called the equator. This part of the earth receives a lot of sunlight no matter how the earth turns, so it is always warm and summerlike in countries on or near the equator. The two halves of the earth above and below the equator are called the Northern and Southern Hemispheres. When the earth is turned so that the Southern Hemisphere receives more sunlight, it is summer there; but at that same time the Northern Hemisphere is in such a position that it gets very little sunlight; days are short and nights are long, so it is winter. In this book it is New Year's Day, and it is cold and snowy in the U.S.A., England, Japan, China, and the U.S.S.R. in the Northern Hemisphere, but warm and sunny in Brazil, Australia, and Kenya in the Southern Hemisphere.

Over the millennia, people have adapted physically to the climatic conditions of the part of the earth they live in. For example, some scientists think adaptation may account for the fact that many people who live in very sunny places have darker skins than those who live in cooler countries—the extra melanin in dark skin helps protect it from possibly harmful effects of the strong sun. People who live in the Andes mountains of Peru usually have rather short, very strong legs, well-suited to climbing the steep slopes. But the reasons for the various racial characteristics are not yet really fully understood. They make people look different, but the differences are superficial, and have nothing to do with intelligence or other personality traits. Fundamentally, we are all very much alike.

—MA

About the Artists

Eric Carle (U.S.A.) was born in the United States in 1929, but later moved with his parents to Germany. He graduated from the Academy of Graphic Arts in Stuttgart. Returning to the United States, he worked for a time in advertising. His first book for children was an immediate success, and was soon followed by his prize-winning classic, *The Very Hungry Caterpillar,* a picturebook beloved by children all over the world. Eric Carle and his wife live in a small hill town in western Massachusetts, U.S.A.

Gian (Gianvittore) Calvi (Brazil) was born in Italy in 1939, but has lived for many years in Brazil. He studied art and industrial design in Rio de Janeiro, and now is involved with many projects in visual communication, with a special dedication to the field of children's books. His books have been published all around the world and he has won several national and international prizes for them. He has also served as advisor on children's book illustration for such international organizations as UNESCO, CERLAL, and PILI. He now lives in Rio de Janeiro, Brazil.

Raymond Briggs (England) was born in Wimbledon in 1934, the son of a milkman (upon whom his famous *Father Christmas* books are based). He studied at the Wimbledon School of Art and later at the Slade School, and then began his career as an illustrator. He was awarded the Kate Greenaway Medal for his *Mother Goose Treasury* in 1966 and again in 1973 for *Father Christmas.* He also won the Francis Williams Award in 1982 for *The Snowman.* He lives in Sussex, England.

Leo and Diane Dillon (Kenya) have won the Caldecott Medal and many other awards for their distinctive and elegant illustrations. They were born only eleven days apart, Leo in New York and Diane in California. They met as students at the Parsons School of Design and the School of Visual Arts, a meeting which led to artistic collaboration and also to marriage. Many of their prize-winning books have had African settings, so it was natural for them to illustrate the sections in this book on Kenya. The Dillons and their son live in Brooklyn, New York, U.S.A.